P9-BIL-793

THE MAGIC BOAT = DEMI

Henry Holt and Company · New York

Published by Henry Holt and Company, Inc., 115 West 18th Street, New York, New York 10011.
Published in Canada by Fitzhenry & Whiteside Limited, 195 Allstate Parkway, Markham, Ontario L3R 4T8.

Library of Congress Cataloging-in-Publication Data
Demi.   The magic boat / by Demi.
Summary: When honest Chang is tricked out of his magic boat, he
and his friends venture to win it back from wicked Ying and the greedy Emperor.
ISBN 0-8050-1141-2   [1. Folklore—China.] I. Title.
PZ8.1.D38Mag 1990 398.21′0951—dc20   [E]   90-4425

First Edition
Designed by Maryann Leffingwell
Printed in the United States of America
1 3 5 7 9 10 8 6 4 2

Once upon a time in China there was a boy named Chang. In Chinese, "Chang" means "honesty," and this boy was well named. He lived with his mother and a big white cat, and he worked hard every day cutting firewood. All agreed that he had a very kind heart.

One day on his way to the mountains to cut wood, Chang saw an old man crossing a bridge made of a single log.

"The bridge is dangerous!" Chang called out, but the old man had already lost his footing and was falling into the river.

Without even taking his clothes off, Chang jumped in after him. He rescued the old man and helped him up onto the riverbank. The old man said, "I am amazed by your courage and selflessness."

He then took from his pocket a little dragon boat. The old man put the boat on the water and whispered, "Grow bigger! Grow bigger! May you brave the wind and water!"

Instantly the little dragon boat turned into a great vessel bobbing on the waves. Then the old man whispered, "Grow smaller! Grow smaller! May you be a toy again!" And immediately the boat shrank back to its original size.

"A magic boat!" cried Chang.

"It is yours," the old man said, handing it to Chang. "If ever you need my help, just turn to the east and call, 'Grandfather! Grandfather!' Remember this—turn east and cry, 'Grandfather! Grandfather!'" And he disappeared into the air.

That evening it began to rain, and it kept raining heavily for ten days and ten nights. When Chang's village began to flood, he took out his little dragon boat and whispered, "Grow bigger! Grow bigger! May you brave the wind and water!" The little boat turned into a great vessel, and Chang climbed aboard with his mother and the big white cat.

The boat had not sailed far before the white cat looked overboard and began to mew. Chang looked too, and saw an ant struggling helplessly in the water. He scooped up the ant and placed him on board. Immediately the little ant picked up an oar and started rowing the boat!

The white cat looked overboard and began to mew again. This time Chang saw a queen bee drowning in the waves. He plucked her from the water and put her in the boat, and no sooner had her wings dried than she began helping with the heavy rudder!

Suddenly a crane, exhausted from a long day's flight, fell into the boat. Chang rushed to the poor bird to see if he could help him, but the crane, having rested a moment, got up and started helping the ant with the oars.

Soon the little crew heard a cry of "Help! Help!" from a man struggling in the water. Without hesitation Chang threw the drowning man a rope and helped him into the magic boat.

"Who are you?" Chang asked the man.

"My name is Ying," he replied. In Chinese, "Ying" means "tricky," and this man was well named. "This is a fine boat," said tricky Ying, "and you are lucky to have such a hardworking man as myself aboard."

But Ying did nothing from the moment he came on board but lie down and give orders, claiming that the long struggle in the water had tired him out.

Little by little the floodwaters went down, and Chang steered back to his village. Then he whispered, "Grow smaller! Grow smaller! May you be a toy again!" and the great vessel was once again a little dragon boat. When Ying saw this, he wanted it for himself, and he began to plot at once.

Chang's house was ruined from the flood. The big white cat, the ant, the queen bee, the crane, and Chang and his mother all set to work building a new one. They carried heavy beams and moved loads of earth, but Ying only gave orders.

One day Ying said, "Everyone knows how hard it is to build a new house. Let me take the magic boat to the Emperor. He will certainly give me gold and silver for it. Then nobody will have to work anymore!"

"But what will we do if there is another flood?" asked Chang.

"Nonsense!" said Ying. "Such a great flood occurs only once every ten thousand years. I will return by nightfall."

Chang believed him and gave him the boat. Greedily snatching it up, Ying made straightaway for the Emperor's palace.

That evening, when Ying failed to return, Chang realized that he had been tricked. He was so filled with rage that he hardly said good-bye to his mother and friends before racing to the capital to retrieve his magic boat.

There were so many people! For ten days and ten nights Chang wandered up and down the streets of the city, searching in vain for tricky Ying.

Then one day he heard trumpets blaring and gongs sounding. Voices shouted, "Make way! Make way! Make way for the new Prime Minister!"

And who was this new Prime Minister? None other than Ying himself!

Chang felt his anger mounting. He stepped forward, barring Ying's procession, and shouted, "Give me back what is mine, you wicked thief!"

Ying was terrified of facing the boy who had saved his life—the boy he had then cheated—and so he ordered several of his guards to take Chang away and beat him.

The white cat, the ant, the queen bee, the crane, and Chang's mother waited for Chang to return. But after many days when he did not come, the animals decided to go to the capital and search for him. After looking for three days and three nights, they finally found him, dirty and bruised, in a little deserted pavillion.

To help Chang recover, the crane caught a great big fish and the white cat brewed a wonderful healing tea, which the queen bee sweetened with her own honey. And best of all, the ant dug up a little red bag full of magic medicine.

At last Chang was well again, and they decided to go to the Emperor and tell him of Ying's wickedness.

But how to gain entrance to the palace? As fate would have it, the Princess had fallen ill, and the Emperor had issued an edict stating that whoever could cure the Princess would be granted one wish.

Chang's friends decided to disguise him as a doctor and go to the palace to cure the Princess.

They arrived at the palace and were soon led to the Emperor. There he sat, surrounded by mountains of food, eating and drinking and amusing himself! Everything was left in the hands of his tricky Prime Minister.

Ying recognized Chang through his disguise. "Your Highness," he said, turning to the Emperor, "I know that this boy is a woodcutter, and not a doctor at all. He and his odd friends should be cast out at once!"

Before the Emperor had a chance to give the order, Chang cried out, "I have magic medicine that can cure the Princess! Please let me prove it."
The Emperor was so anxious to have her recover that he agreed.

As soon as the Princess appeared, Chang took out the little red bag of magic medicine and sprinkled the powder all over her. The Princess miraculously recovered!

The Emperor was so happy, he said to Chang, "Whatever you choose is yours."

Chang answered, "All I ask is the return of my magic boat."

But the magic boat had brought great fame to the Emperor, and he was unwilling to give up his prize so easily. "Wait a minute," he told Chang. "I must confer with my Prime Minister about your request."

Ying quickly whispered a devious plot into the Emperor's ear.

He suggested that the Princess and seven of her maids wear identical dresses and cover their faces with identical veils. Chang was to pick which of the eight was the Princess. If he guessed right, the magic boat was his; if he guessed wrong, he would lose it forever.

Chang was distressed, but the queen bee whispered to him, "Don't worry. Only the Princess will be wearing fresh flowers in her hair. The others' will be made of paper. I will show you which to pick."

When the time came for Chang to choose, the queen bee buzzed around the head of the real Princess, and Chang easily picked her out.

Again the greedy Emperor went back on his word. He said, "I will give you a piece of gold instead!" But Chang refused, insisting on the magic boat that was rightfully his. Unsure of what to do, the Emperor turned to Ying for help once more.

"Prove to the Emperor that the magic boat is yours," Ying said.

The animals didn't know what to do, but Chang, remembering the words of the old man, turned to the east and called, "Grandfather! Grandfather!"

At these words thunder sounded and the old man appeared, riding a golden phoenix. He said to the Emperor and Ying, "It was I who rewarded Chang with the magic boat!"

But still they would not give up their prize.

The crane then shouted, "Tricky Ying is a mean, bad man! Turn him into an old gray wolf!" The other animals jumped up and down in approval.

The old man whispered, "One, two, three, four, five, six, seven. Tricky Ying is an old gray wolf!"

Seeing Ying's fate, the Emperor tried to escape, but he was too fat to go very far. The ant shouted, "The Emperor is a greedy man! Turn him into a big wild pig!"

The old man whispered, "One, two, three, four, five, six, seven. The Emperor is a big wild pig!"

Chang and his friends retrieved the magic boat and happily returned home to Chang's mother. In times of trouble they used the magic boat to help those in distress, and in times of peace they used it to bring joy!